R0083794446

Jon Scieszka's TRUCKTOWN
KAT'S MYSTERY GIFT

WRITTEN BY JON SCIESZKA

CHARACTERS AND ENVIRONMENTS DEVELOPED BY THE

DAVID SHANNON   **LOREN LONG**   **DAVID GORDON**

ILLUSTRATION CREW:

Executive producer: Keytoon, Inc. in association with Animagic S.L.

Creative supervisor: Sergio Pablos ○ Drawings by: Juan Pablo Navas ○ Color by: Isabel Nadal

Color assistant: Gabriela Lazbal ○ Art director: Karin Paprocki

READY-TO-READ

SIMON SPOTLIGHT
NEW YORK   LONDON   TORONTO   SYDNEY

ABDO
Spotlight

ABDOPUBLISHING.COM

Reinforced library bound edition published
in 2016 by Spotlight, a division of ABDO.
PO Box 398166, Minneapolis, Minnesota 55439.
Spotlight produces high-quality reinforced library
bound editions for schools and libraries.
Published by agreement with Simon Spotlight.

Printed in the United States of America, North Mankato, Minnesota.
042015   092015

SIMON SPOTLIGHT
An imprint of Simon & Schuster Children's Publishing Division
1230 Avenue of the Americas, New York, NY 10020
First Simon Spotlight paperback edition June 2008

LIBRARY OF CONGRESS CATALOGING-IN-PUBLICATION DATA

This title was previously cataloged with the following information:

Scieszka, Jon.
 Kat's mystery gift / written by Jon Scieszka ; characters and environments developed by
Design Garage: David Shannon, Loren Long, David Gordon. — 1st Aladdin Paperbacks ed.
 p. cm. — (Trucktown) (Ready-to-roll)
Summary: the trucks speculate about what could be inside a beautifully wrapped gift box.
[1. Gifts—Fiction. 2. Trucks—Fiction.] I. Design Garage. II. Title.
PZ7.S41267Kat 2009
[E]—dc22
                2007027801
978-1-61479-396-0 (reinforced library bound edition)

THIS BOOK CONTAINS
RECYCLED MATERIAL

Spotlight   A Division of ABDO   abdopublishing.com

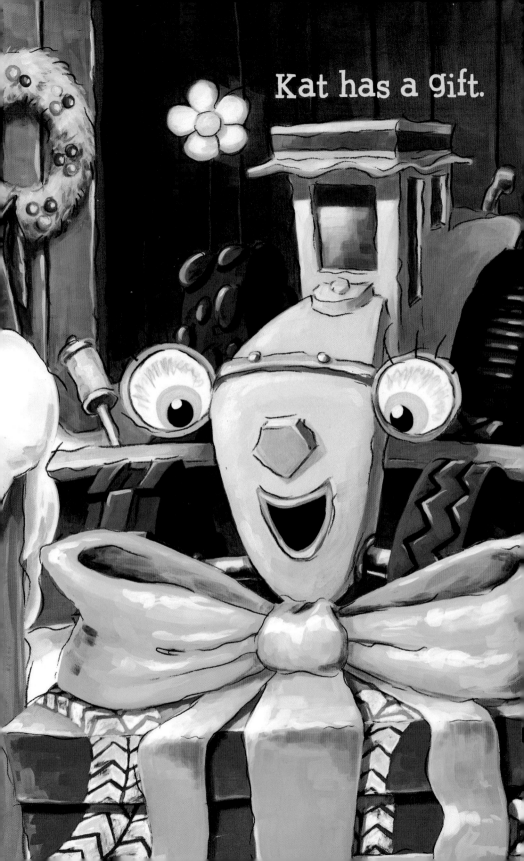

Kat has a gift.

The gift is red.

"I guess it is a new horn,"
says Gabby.
"Could be," says Kat.

"I guess it is a new ball," says Rosie.

"Could be," says Kat.

"I guess it
is new tires,"
says Pete.

"New sirens?" guesses Pat.
"New lights?" guesses Lucy.

"But it could be a jewel," says Kat.

"Or a cloud..."

"WOW!"

says Gabby.

"Open it, open it,
open it now!"
they all cheer.
"We could . . . ," says Kat.